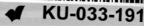

DOG POWDER

MARY HOFFMAN

Illustrated by
PAUL WARREN

HEINEMANN · LONDON

For the girls, particularly Jessica,
who gave me the title

William Heinemann Ltd
Michelin House, 81 Fulham Road,
London SW3 6RB

LONDON MELBOURNE AUCKLAND

First published 1989
Text © 1989 Mary Hoffmann
Illustrations © 1989 Paul Warren

ISBN 0 434 93059 8
Printed in Hong Kong by
Mandarin Offset

A school pack of SUPERCHAMPS 1–6
is available from
Heinemann Educational Books
ISBN 0 435 00090 X

1 Rover

PARROTT'S PET SHOP didn't have any
pets. Perhaps that's why Colin liked it
so much. He didn't have any pets
either. They weren't allowed in the flats
where he lived. NO PETS, NO BALL
GAMES and NO WALKING ON THE
GRASS. The only animal on the whole
estate was Major, the caretaker's dog.
Major Disaster, Colin's dad called him.
He was a dark brown Doberman and
very fierce.

'He's supposed to be fierce,' said Mr Webster, the caretaker. 'Major is a guard-dog, not a pet. He's not the kind of dog you pat or throw balls for.' But a dog you pat and throw balls for was just the kind of pet that a lot of the children on the estate really wanted. Particularly Colin.

Colin's family thought he was slightly mad. He had invented a dog called Rover, who went everywhere with him. It was a medium sized mongrel with a brown shaggy coat. He tied his invisible dog up outside food shops, played invisible football with him in the park and let him sleep, invisibly, at the end of the bed. He believed in Rover so completely that it was *almost* as good as having a real dog. He forgot that other people couldn't see Rover and he was always getting into trouble with

Mr Webster. The caretaker was always suspicious that people might be secretly keeping dogs on the estate.

One day Colin was whistling and throwing a ball for Rover in the yard when Mr Webster pounced.

'Gotcha this time, young Piper,' he said fiercely. 'Where is it?'

Colin blushed. For a moment he felt he really *had* been caught with a dog – after all, he could see Rover sitting patiently, waiting for him to throw the ball again. But Mr Webster was looking round impatiently at the empty yard.

'Where's the dog you were playing with?' he barked.

But Colin wasn't going to tell Mr Webster his dog was imaginary. In the end he had to let Colin go, but he confiscated his ball all the same.

'He must have a mountain of them in his flat,' thought Colin gloomily.

Next morning Colin asked his older brother Nick to take Rover for a walk when he went on his paper-round, because he was too busy to take him himself.

'Colin's bonkers about that dog,' Nick told their sister, Clare.

'What dog?' said Clare.

'You know, Rover,' said Nick.

'It's you who's bonkers,' said Clare, 'there isn't any Rover.'

'You know what I mean,' said Nick crossly. 'He's even started to buy things for it.'

And he had. Ever since Mr Parrott had opened his pet shop in the little row of shops round the corner from the flats, Colin had been popping in there almost every day. Although Mr Parrott didn't sell pets, he sold practically everything else: daffodil bulbs and dibbers, dustbins and dusters and, of course, everything you could possibly need for a dog. Colin spent hours among the collars and toy bones, the sacks of dog biscuits and tins of flea powder. Rover

never felt so real as when he waited
patiently outside Parrott's Pet Shop, for
Colin to come out.

Colin and Mr Parrott were great
friends. They shared a secret. Mr

Parrott couldn't have pets either. He had terrible asthma and wasn't allowed to keep a cat or a dog.

'Not even a bird,' confided Mr Parrott to Colin. 'No, I'm the only Parrott in this shop and the only one there ever will be. But if I can't have a pet, a pet-shop's the next best thing.'

Although Mr Parrott's shop was so new, all the things in it looked rather old and musty, like Mr Parrott himself. The shelves were cluttered with odd tins and jars, some with labels half-missing or unreadable with rust-spots.

'That shop's downright unhygienic,' Colin's mother said. She didn't like him spending so much time there.

'That's why I like it,' said Colin. 'You never know what you might find there!'

'Hmph,' snorted his mother. 'Something catching, I expect.'

But Colin kept going to Mr Parrott's. He bought a collar and lead for Rover, and a medallion with his name and address on it. And he was saving up for a proper dog bed. Soon he took to dropping in on Mr Parrott every day after school for a chat.

Mr Parrott knew about Rover. Rover was the only dog who didn't make him sneeze. He and Colin never mentioned the fact that Rover wasn't really there. But sometimes they exchanged looks of understanding doglessness. Mr Parrott was sorry for Colin and Colin was sorry for Mr Parrott.

'He's a funny old bloke, your Parrott,' said Nick. 'Looks a bit like a wizard, with that little white beard of his, and the funny black cap he wears.'

'How many wizards do you know then, Nick?' retorted Colin. He always got angry if anyone teased him about Mr Parrott.

'All right, keep your hair on,' said Nick. 'He's quite a nice old boy, I expect. But you've got to admit, he does look a bit odd.'

'No odder than your friends who go round with their hair bright pink or green,' said Colin, but he knew Nick was right. Mr Parrott *was* different from other people. He understood Colin, for a start.

But he was different in other ways, too. He seemed to be able to make things appear and disappear. Not just the ordinary sort of tricks with cards or eggcups that you see on TV, but really amazing things. He would only do them when there was no-one else but Colin in the shop. But he could make a bunch of real flowers appear out of a tin of dog food and once, he was fiddling with a ball of green garden twine when it suddenly seemed to turn into a freshly-baked cherry cake.

One day in the summer holidays, Colin was feeling fed up. He mooched slowly along the street, Rover at his heels. He had met a boy he knew in the newsagents and he had a mongrel puppy with him. This boy lived in a house. Not a grand or large house, but a house

all the same with a little garden, where there were no notices saying NO. Suddenly Rover didn't seem much of a dog compared with that warm plump puppy looking adoringly up into its master's face. Then Colin felt a bit guilty. It wasn't Rover's fault. He was as real as he could be.

'Come on boy,' said Colin. 'Let's go and see Mr Parrott.'

Mr Parrott saw straight away that Colin was depressed.

'Come over and look at the dog things,' he said. 'I've just had another delivery.'

Colin sometimes wondered where Mr Parrott's stock came from. It all looked second hand. This time there were a lot of dingy old cans and sprays that looked as if they were well past any 'sell by' date. Mr Parrott picked up what

looked like a tin of talcum powder and
handed it to Colin. 'Now this is the sort
of thing that might interest you, Colin,'
he said, peering down at the tin through
his half-moon glasses. 'This is very
difficult stuff to get a-hold of
nowadays.'

Colin looked at the tin. The lid had holes that you turned to match another set of holes underneath. There was a label but it was very stained and torn.

Colin read what was left:

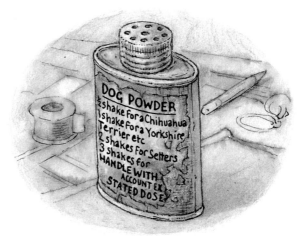

DOG POWDER
½ shake for a Chihuahua
1 shake for a Yorkshire
Terrier etc
2 shakes for Setters
3 shakes for
HANDLE WITH
ACCOUNT EX
STATED DOSE

The tin felt good and solid in his hand. Colin wondered how you gave it half a shake.

'What's it for, Mr Parrott?' he asked.

'Ah-ha,' said Mr Parrott. 'I don't rightly know exactly *what* it's for, but I think *who* it's for may be you. Only you've got to be careful with it and follow the instructions.' Just then he had to stop and serve Mrs Evans who always came in on Wednesdays to buy food for Mitzi, her pekinese. While she dithered over the dog biscuits Colin made up his mind.

'How much is the Dog Powder, Mr Parrott?' he asked.

'Oh, mmm, to you fifty pence,' said the old man absent-mindedly. 'Yes, I like the shape of those fifty pences.'

Colin handed him one and he looked at it for a long time before Mrs Evans called him over again.

'Oh, and Colin,' he called after him as the boy left the shop. 'I don't think I told you. It's a "dawn to dusk" powder.'

Colin shrugged his shoulders as he left the shop. Mr Parrott certainly was an unusual friend.

2 Etcetera

COLIN'S DAD HAD the next day off and
they were going to the seaside for an
outing. They all squashed into their old
car, carrying swimsuits, towels and bags
of food. It was a tight squeeze with the
three children in the back. Dad looked
round at them before setting off.

'I'll say one thing for that dog of
yours, Colin,' he said, 'he takes up less
room than most!'

Nick and Clare laughed but Colin sat
unsmiling in the middle, Rover on his
knee. He had Rover's collar and lead
with him and just before they had left
the flat, he had found himself slipping
Mr Parrott's tin of dog-powder into his
anorak pocket. He could feel it sticking
into him now.

Just before they got to Heathcliff-on-sea Colin had to take the tin of powder out of his pocket because it was digging into his leg. He held it on his lap, fiddling with the top and looking out at the leafy lanes. Suddenly Dad swerved to avoid a cyclist and Colin found some powder had spilt out of the tin. In a split second there was a small black-and-white dog on Colin's knee.

Colin couldn't believe his eyes; nor could Clare and Nick. Mum and Dad were arguing about the cyclist so they didn't notice anything.

'One shake for a Yorkshire terrier etc.,' thought Colin. 'This must be the etc.' And straight away he named this miraculous dog Etcetera, because he looked like a mixture of leftover bits of other dogs. But it was a real enough result. Etcetera looked up at Colin and licked his nose. Clare and Nick were still sitting frozen in amazement with their mouths open and their eyes glazed. Colin frowned and shook his head at them. He didn't know exactly how it had happened or how long it would last, but he wasn't going to have them spoiling his best chance of having a real live dog. Then Etcetera began to bark and whimper excitedly. Colin held his breath. Dad was guiding the car through the winding streets of Heathcliff and Mum was looking for the car park but even so they couldn't be expected not to notice a dog barking in the back of the car.

'Your imitations get more lifelike every day, Colin,' said Mum, peering out of her window.

'Cut it out, Col,' said Dad.

With one accord, the three children entered into an instant pact to keep their parents from noticing the dog from nowhere. Colin took off his anorak and wrapped it round Etcetera in a bundle. Clare fed him with chocolate buttons every time he looked as if he might bark and Nick engaged their parents in bright and useful conversation about the nearest place to the beach where they could park. They found a car park right up on the dunes above the beach and in the confusion of unpacking the car it was easy for Colin to run on ahead with his armful of secret dog.

It was the best day on the beach he had ever had. Mum did wonder a bit about the little black-and-white dog who kept getting Colin to throw sticks into the sea for him.

'Who does it belong to?' asked Mum. 'No-one seems to be looking for it.'

'You know who I reckon it is?' said Dad, settling down for a snooze after lunch. 'I reckon it's that Rover that Colin brought down in the car!' And he chuckled at his own joke.

Nick and Clare tackled Colin as soon as they had all run, with Etcetera at their heels, down to the sea and out of earshot of their parents. He explained as best he could about Mr Parrott's dog powder but he could see they didn't believe him.

'Are you trying to tell me,' said Clare, 'that this dog came out of a tin?'

'What *I* can't figure out,' said Nick, 'is how you managed to smuggle him into the car without us seeing *and* keep him quiet till we were nearly here.'

Colin gave up trying to convince them and concentrated on having his own dog to play with. But at the back of his mind he couldn't forget the journey back to London. How would he get Etcetera back in the car? He couldn't just abandon him in Heathcliff. It was a long sunny day, one of the best that summer. Mum and Dad were in no particular hurry to get back because

they wanted to avoid the worst of the traffic: it was Mum's turn to drive on the way back.

'We'll pick up some fish and chips half way,' Dad said, as they eventually started to pack up.

'You'll have to take that dog to the beach attendant, Colin,' said Mum, pulling on her cardigan. There weren't many people left on the beach now and, naturally, no-one claimed Etcetera. Nick and Clare exchanged desperate looks as Colin set off miserably with the little dog in his arms. The sun was setting behind the dunes.

'That boy's dog crazy,' said Mum on the way back to the car park. 'It's a shame we can't let him have one.'

'It is,' said Dad,' but we're lucky to have a roof over our heads and me still in work, the rate they're making people redundant at the factory. Don't forget the lights,' he added, 'it must be lighting-up time now.'

Down on the beach Colin felt the little black-and-white dog tremble in his arms. It licked his nose and then it was gone. All that was left was a light dusting of white powder on the front of Colin's anorak.

'Dawn to dusk,' thought Colin. 'Is that what Mr Parrott meant?' As he ran back to the car he didn't know whether to laugh or cry.

3 Blue

'GO ON THEN – I dare you!' said Nick.

The three children were standing in the yard where people hung out their washing behind the flats. Colin was holding the tin of powder in one hand and glaring at his brother and sister. All of a sudden, he didn't care what happened. He twisted the lid and gave the tin two good shakes onto the floor of the yard. Instantly, a handsome red setter stood before them.

'Blimey!' said Nick, goggle eyed.

Clare sat down hard and suddenly on the concrete. Colin felt a surge of triumph. He hadn't been sure if the powder would work again.

'Here!' he called and the dog wagged

27

its tail and thrust its long red muzzle
into Colin's hand.

'Oy! Get that dog out of here!' yelled
a loud voice. 'You know the rules!' It
was Mr Webster. He came puffing and
wheezing round the corner. Luckily for
them he didn't have Major with him.

'It's not ours,' said Nick quickly.

'No, it just appeared out of nowhere,'
added Clare and then got a fit of giggles.
Mr Webster looked suspicious.

'So you don't know anything about
it?' he said, looking hard at Colin. He
was sure he had tracked down Colin's
mystery dog at last.

'Honest,' said Colin, 'I've never seen
it before in my life.'

The setter stood up on its back legs
wagging its feathery tail, put its front
paws on Colin's shoulders and started to

give him a good wash. Mr Webster snorted.

'Looks like it, doesn't it? Well whoever's it is, get it out of here before I report you to the Council.'

They went. Colin's new red setter followed obediently at his heels. They went to the park but they could see they were going to have a problem. It was only ten o'clock in the morning and it wouldn't be lighting-up time until nearly nine o'clock that night.

'I think we're going to be stuck with him until it gets dark,' explained Colin. 'At least, if he's like the last one. At dusk, he'll just turn back into two shakes of dog powder.'

'But we can't stay in the park all day,' objected Clare. 'Mum and Dad would go spare.'

'Besides, we'll get hungry,' said Nick, 'if we can't go back for dinner.'

'You go back,' said Colin. 'Tell Mum and Dad I've gone to spend the day with a friend. I'll stay out here with Blue.'

'Blue?' said Nick. 'What kind of name is that for a red setter?'

'An unusual one,' said Colin, 'and you've got to admit he's an unusual dog.'

They all looked at Blue, who was following their conversation with an intelligent look. They had been so busy worrying about the caretaker that they hadn't had time to think about the dog himself, who was so solid and real but who simply hadn't existed before they went out into the yard that morning. Nick and Clare looked at Colin with new respect. It made them feel differently about Mr Parrott, too.

'I wonder if he's got any cat powder,'

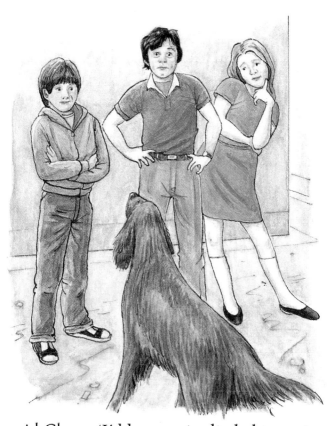

said Clare. 'I'd love a nice little kitten.'

'Why not go the whole hog and ask for a tin of instant horse?' asked Nick. He was a bit jealous of Colin's new-found powers.

'Look, stop arguing, you two,' said Colin. 'You go home and tell Mum and Dad I'm not coming home till late. You can come back and find me in the park after dinner.'

But that wasn't how things worked out. Colin had a marvellous morning with Blue, running and jumping and throwing sticks. Then they got hungry and Colin slipped Rover's collar and lead onto Blue's neck and took him to buy hamburgers. After they had eaten, Colin felt at a bit of a loose end. He would have liked to lie on his bed and read his comics, with Blue snoozing at his feet. But he knew it would be too dangerous to sneak the dog into the flats while Mr Webster was on the war-path. So he mooched lazily back to the park and that was where he felt the first large spots of rain. It was a violent summer thunderstorm, the kind that often happens after weeks of hot weather. Colin was soon soaked to the skin.

'Here, boy,' he said to Blue, who was equally bedraggled and miserable. 'I'd like a hot bath and some dry clothes, wouldn't you?' Blue shook his wet ears.

'No, I don't suppose you would. Dogs hate baths. But they hate being out in the rain, too. I don't know what to do.'

He bent down and rubbed Blue's head.

'Yes I do, I'm going back to Mr Parrott to ask for a powder to make dogs disappear. I hate to do it to you, Blue, but I don't think you can take much more of this.'

They ran to Mr Parrott's and Colin regretfully tied Blue up outside.

'You're real enough to make

Mr Parrott sneeze,' he told him. 'But I won't be long.'

He dived through the shop door making the bell jingle violently. Blue looked after him with sad brown eyes, his tail between his legs. Then along the street came Mr Webster holding a huge umbrella over himself and Major, the giant Doberman.

4   Major Disaster

'YOU'VE GOT TO help me, Mr Parrott,'
said Colin desperately. 'Blue hates being
out in the rain and there's nowhere I can
take him without being caught.'

Mr Parrott looked very serious.

'What you are asking for is very
dangerous, Colin,' he said. 'I never
normally sell it over the counter. Just
think of the problems it could cause if
wrongly used!'

'*Please*, Mr Parrott,' begged Colin.

'Oh, all right,' said the old man, 'but I didn't think you'd be asking for something to get rid of dogs so soon.'

'Mr Parrott, it's been magic,' said Colin, his eyes shining. 'I've had two wonderful dogs and next time I'll be more careful, I promise. The next dog will be at the right time in the right place. But Blue was, well, just to show my brother and sister how the powder worked.'

'Ah,' said Mr Parrott, 'you did not "handle with care", as instructed?' Colin shook his head. Mr Parrott handed him a smaller tin without any label at all.

'You just use the same directions as on the other tin. "Half a shake for a chihuahua" and so on,' said Mr Parrott. 'But it is even more important not to exceed the stated dose. If you shook *three* shakes over a chihuahua, for instance, you'd have about one Great Dane's worth of vanishing powder left over. It would make a kind of Black Hole you couldn't see – and the next dog who came along would be sucked into it.' Colin was hardly listening. He had an awful feeling that something bad was about to happen to Blue, something worse than being sent back to where he had come from. He almost snatched the tin from Mr Parrott and, shouting his thanks, ran out of the shop. Just in time to see Mr Webster bending over Blue and reading the name and address on his medallion:

What happened next was difficult for Colin to describe afterwards because a lot of different things happened at once. Blue saw Colin and wagged his wet tail. Mr Webster saw Colin and began to shout. Major saw Mr Webster beginning to shout at Colin, so he began

to growl. Blue objected to Major
growling at Colin and began to bark.
Colin lunged at Blue with the tin of
dog-dispeller, but he was so worried
about the amount that he missed. He
didn't have time to worry about a 'black
hole' or anything because Major dashed

at Blue with all his teeth showing and Blue managed to unhook his lead and bolted for the park. Major, Colin and Mr Webster all ran after him.

As he ran to the park, Colin twisted the lid round on the tin of dog-dispeller and held his hand firmly over the top.

'I must get it right this time,' he thought. 'If Mr Webster catches Blue, with Rover's medallion on, I've had my chips.'

He dashed through the gates, just behind the furious Major and several yards ahead of Mr Webster, who wasn't nearly as fit. By the water fountain, Blue turned and faced his enemy. Both dogs circled one another stiff-legged. They were fairly evenly matched in size and it was going to be quite a battle.

'Now or never,' thought Colin and dashed in with the tin. As he was holding it over Blue, Major made his first move. He flung himself at Blue, teeth snapping. Colin spun round and the two shakes of dog-dispeller landed neatly on Major's back. Mr Webster came puffing through the gates just in time to see his dog disappear into thin air.

5 Minus Dog

THE NEXT FEW hours were the worst in
Colin's life. The only good thing was
that the rain stopped. Mr Webster had
been running so fast that he couldn't
stop and tripped over Blue's lead at the
same time as Colin grabbed it. He went
down like a skittle and banged his head
on the drinking fountain.

Just then Nick and Clare arrived.
They didn't know what was up but they
could see it would be a good idea for
Colin to go. Colin, shaking from head to
foot, took Blue out of the other side of
the park and onto a K7 bus. They sat
upstairs and went to the end of the bus's
route and back again three times in total
silence. Luckily Colin had enough

money on him to keep paying for the bus fares. Blue seemed as stunned by the sudden disappearance of Major as Colin and Mr Webster had been. In his head, Colin kept seeing newspaper headlines:

'Boy Spirits Dog Away!'

'Vandal Sent to Borstal for Wiping Out Caretaker's Dog.'

This was the worst scrape he had ever been in.

Colin listed all the points in his mind over and over again.

1 He couldn't go home till nearly 9 o'clock.

2 He didn't know if Mr Webster was badly hurt.

3 He didn't know if Major would ever return, or would stay disappeared, like Etcetera.

4 He didn't dare try the dog-dispeller

on Blue a third time – he had lost
his nerve.

5 He had just remembered that this
was Wednesday afternoon and
Mrs Evans would be going to the
pet shop with Mitzi and would tie
her up exactly where he had
thrown the vanishing powder.

6 He was going to get into the most
unholy row with Mum and Dad,
just over 1, let alone 2, 3, 4 and 5.

At 8.30 Colin and Blue got off the bus
and walked slowly back through the
park. They both stopped at the fountain
and exchanged mournful looks. Colin
patted Blue's head. He was a super dog
and it was awful to think, in addition to
all his other problems, that in less than
half an hour Blue just wouldn't be there
any more. As they got nearer to the
flats Colin's heart sank lower and lower.

Blue pressed against his leg. He turned
the corner of his block just as the sun set
and ran into a reception committee. At
the front was Mr Webster, perfectly all
right but very angry. Colin just heard
him say,

'You see, I *told* you the little blighter had a dog,' as he felt the warm pressure of Blue's side suddenly lift.

'Goodbye, Blue,' said Colin softly, and then chaos broke out around him. His mother was crying as she hugged him and shouted at him at the same time. His father looked stern and white-faced. Only Nick and Clare looked pleased to see Colin. There were two other people there. One was PC Link and the other was someone Colin didn't know, a man in a business suit.

'Look,' said Dad, 'let's all get inside and have a drink. Whatever this young man's done, he's clearly exhausted and needs warming up.'

They all trooped into Colin's flat. Nick told him what was going on while he changed into his pyjamas and a big thick sweater.

'There's been hell to pay here,' said Nick. 'As soon as old Webster came round, he went straight round to the cop-shop and said he was going to sue Mum and Dad because you stole his dog.'

'Crikey,' groaned Colin, towelling his damp hair.

'*Then* he went down to the Housing Department and told this geezer, Mr Snow, that you were keeping a dog in the flats. Here, by the way, what happened to Blue?'

'He . . . you know – like the other one,' said Colin, trying not to sound too choked.

'Too bad,' said Nick, sympathetically, 'but in the circumstances, he couldn't have made a better move. They won't be able to prove a thing now.'

'Did you see him, just as we got back?' asked Colin.

'No,' said Nick, 'the sun was in my eyes.'

The boys went back into the living room, where Mr Webster, Mum and PC Link were having a cup of tea. Dad and Mr Snow each had a glass of something stronger and they both looked as if they needed it. Mum made Colin drink a mug of hot, sweet tea before she would let him answer any questions.

Mr Webster was boiling with impatience and soon burst out,

'Aren't you going to do anything? This boy, this family has been blatantly breaking the rules of this estate and to make matters worse, he has made off with my dog, who is a pedigree Doberman Pinscher. I'm going to take them all to court –'

'All right, Mr Webster,' said PC Link. 'The rules of the estate are not my concern. That's Mr Snow's department. But stealing a dog is a serious matter. In fact this is the second missing dog case I've had today.'

'Oh no!' thought Colin. 'I bet the other one was Mitzi!'

'But if you don't mind, I'd like to ask the questions.' PC Link went on, 'I know Colin and I don't think he'd lie to me.'

Colin braced himself.

'Now then, lad,' said PC Link, 'you tell us in your own words what happened. Do you know where Mr Webster's dog is?'

'No sir,' said Colin truthfully.

They all heard the sound of distant barking at the same time.

'Now tell me, Colin,' said PC Link, 'have you got a dog of your own?'

'No sir,' said Colin again.

The barking was nearer now. Mr Webster burst out angrily,

'I saw it three times today. Once outside the flats and once outside that dirty old pet shop. I looked at its medallion and it said "Rover" and this address!'

Mum and Dad burst out laughing at the same time.

'That's one dog you haven't seen,' said Dad and explained to PC Link and Mr Snow:

'Colin's got a game he plays of having a pretend dog called Rover. He's got a collar and lead for it and a name tag. It's a harmless enough game, isn't it, for a lad who can't keep his own pet?'

There was a furious barking at the door of the flat, and something started scratching to come in.

'And what about just now?' demanded Mr Webster, 'He had a dog when he came round the corner and I bet that's it outside the door now.'

'I didn't see any dog just now,' said PC Link. 'But let's go and see who this is at the door.'

They all trooped into the hall and Mr Webster triumphantly opened the door. And into the hall with a volley of barks exploded Major.

6 Gradual Dog

'HERE, COLIN,' SAID Clare, 'Mr Parrott's selling his shop.'

It was the first thing that Colin had paid any attention to since the day that Major had disappeared and returned so dramatically.

'What d'you mean?' he said stupidly.

'It says CLOSING DOWN SALE in the window,' said Clare. 'You'd better go and see him.'

Mum and Dad were too worried to mind if Colin went out or not. Dad had been made redundant the day after the Major incident, which was why Colin hadn't got into as much trouble as he had expected. They hardly looked up from the jobs column of the newspaper as he called out:

'Going to see Mr Parrott, OK?'

Mr Parrott was reading the newspaper,
surrounded by cardboard boxes.

'Ah, Colin!' he said. 'I was hoping
you'd drop by.'

'What's happened?' asked Colin.
'Why are you closing the shop?'

'I'm going away for a spell, Colin,' he

said. 'I think I've done as much as I can here. Too much, perhaps.'

Colin nodded miserably. He put his hands into his pockets and put the two tins on Mr Parrott's counter.

'You were right,' he said. 'They're both too dangerous.'

He knew he didn't have to explain about Major and Blue.

Mr Parrott brought out a handsome dog-bed from under the counter.

'Would you like this half price?' he said. 'I won't be here long enough for you to save up for it at the full sum.'

Colin just about had enough and Mr Parrott wrapped the bed up carefully for him.

'When are you going?' asked Colin, not really wanting to know the answer.

'Oh, it'll take a few weeks yet, to clear up,' said Mr Parrott.

Back at the flats all was gloom. Term started next week, and all the children had grown out of last winter's clothes. Dad was out of work and there was hardly any to be had around their way. They were sitting silently eating their

tea when the doorbell rang. It was
Mr Snow, the Housing Officer.

'Oh no,' groaned Colin under his
breath.

But Mr Snow was very friendly.

'How's Rover?' he asked Colin,
giving him a wink.

'I hear you've had some bad news,
Mr Piper,' he said to Dad. 'Sorry about
the job, but I've got a suggestion to
make to you. Your caretaker here, Mr
Webster, has decided to retire.'

Colin looked at Nick and Clare and
they made silent cheering noises.

'Yes,' said Mr Snow, 'he's not been
in good health for some time and his
wife was quite worried about
those . . . er . . . hallucinations he had
last week. Anyway, they're moving
down to the coast to live with
Mrs Webster's sister.'

'What about Major?' Colin couldn't help asking.

'Oh, Major's going too. Mrs Webster's sister is a widow and she's had a couple of burglaries recently. She likes the idea of a good guard dog.'

Mr Snow paused. 'The point of telling you all this is that we'll need a new caretaker. The Websters want to move out as soon as possible, so it would be a great help to me if I could find someone nearby who could move into their flat quickly. I was wondering if *you'd* be interested in applying for the job, Mr Piper? You'd be doing me a favour.'

The next few weeks were very busy. As soon as Major and his owners moved out, Mum and Dad were in the caretaker's flat measuring and planning and clearing out all the confiscated footballs. On moving day, a chain of friends could be seen winding across the estate carrying boxes and furniture. Dad was busy re-hanging curtains while Mum brewed up endless pots of tea.

The next morning Colin woke up in his new bedroom feeling very strange. He had been woken by the doorbell. He got up to find Dad letting in Mr Parrott. Colin immediately felt guilty. He hadn't been to see Mr Parrott since the day he took the dog powder back. Mr Parrott was talking to Dad in a low voice. He had something in a box in his arms and he was holding a big white handkerchief over his nose.

'Here, Colin,' said Dad, 'special delivery for you!'

'Colin,' said Mr Parrott, 'your father called in on me a few weeks ago and asked me if I could get a-hold of a dog suitable for a caretaker's family on a large estate.'

He opened the box and a black and white Border Collie pup looked enquiringly up at Colin. He was like a

mixture of Etcetera, Blue and Rover
rolled into one. Colin couldn't believe
his eyes.

'Mr Parrott, you didn't . . . ?'

'Oh no!' said Mr Parrott. 'This is a
gradual dog.'

Colin understood.

'You'll have to look after it,' said Dad,
'I don't know anything about dogs.'

'Thanks, Dad,' said Colin. 'Thanks,
Mr Parrott.'

'Shall we show him the bed?' said
Mr Parrott and they took the little
puppy into Colin's bedroom.

'What will you call him?' asked
Mr Parrott.

Colin thought for a bit. He thought of
how this was a real dog that wouldn't
disappear at the end of the day. And he
thought of all the other dogs Mr Parrott
had tried to give him.

'I shall call him Wizard,' he said. Mr Parrott smiled.

'I've come to say goodbye, too, Colin,' he said. 'I'm leaving today.'

Colin wanted to give him a goodbye present. He opened his top drawer and took out Rover's collar and lead.

'I'd like you to have Rover, Mr Parrott,' he said. '*He* won't make you sneeze. Look after him for me.'

Mr Parrott was delighted. As Colin let him out of the flat, holding Wizard in his arms, he saw Mr Parrott wave. Then Mr Parrott held out the collar and lead and traced the silvery outline of a dog on the empty air. For a few seconds Colin saw Rover for the first and last time. Then they both disappeared.

Every Christmas Colin still gets a card from Mr Parrott with a message about

Rover:

> *Happy Christmas from Mr Parrott.*
> *P.S. Rover well.*

Because one of the many good things about imaginary dogs is that they never grow old and die.